I0703419

The Stork Never Came

A children's book
about pregnancy loss

Jess Voepel

Illustrated by: Alexis St.Clair

ISBN 978-1-956001-43-3 (hardback)
ISBN 978-1-956001-44-0 (eBook)

Printed in the United States of America

*We dedicate this to all angel
babies in Heaven…
And their families still here on Earth.*

My mommy had a baby growing inside her tummy.

I was going to be a big sister.

Then one day, when I came home from school, I saw Mommy crying with what was going to be the new baby's blanket.

When I asked Daddy why Mommy was sad, he told me she had miscarried.

"What does that mean?" I asked.

"A miscarriage means the baby stopped growing," Daddy explained, sadly. "It means the baby is in Heaven now."

"Like Papa?"

Daddy nodded. "Yes, like Papa. Papa will take care of the baby now."

"Daddy?" I asked.

"Yes?" He replied.

"Why did the baby go to Heaven? What was wrong?"

He paused to think for a moment. Then he said, "It is very important for you to understand that it's nobody's fault. Sometimes sad things like this happen, but that doesn't mean someone did something wrong. There wasn't anything Mommy, or anyone, could have done. Nobody is to blame, okay?" I nodded and he continued. "Do you remember last spring when we planted lots of Daisy seeds and only a few sprouted?"

"Yes," I answered.

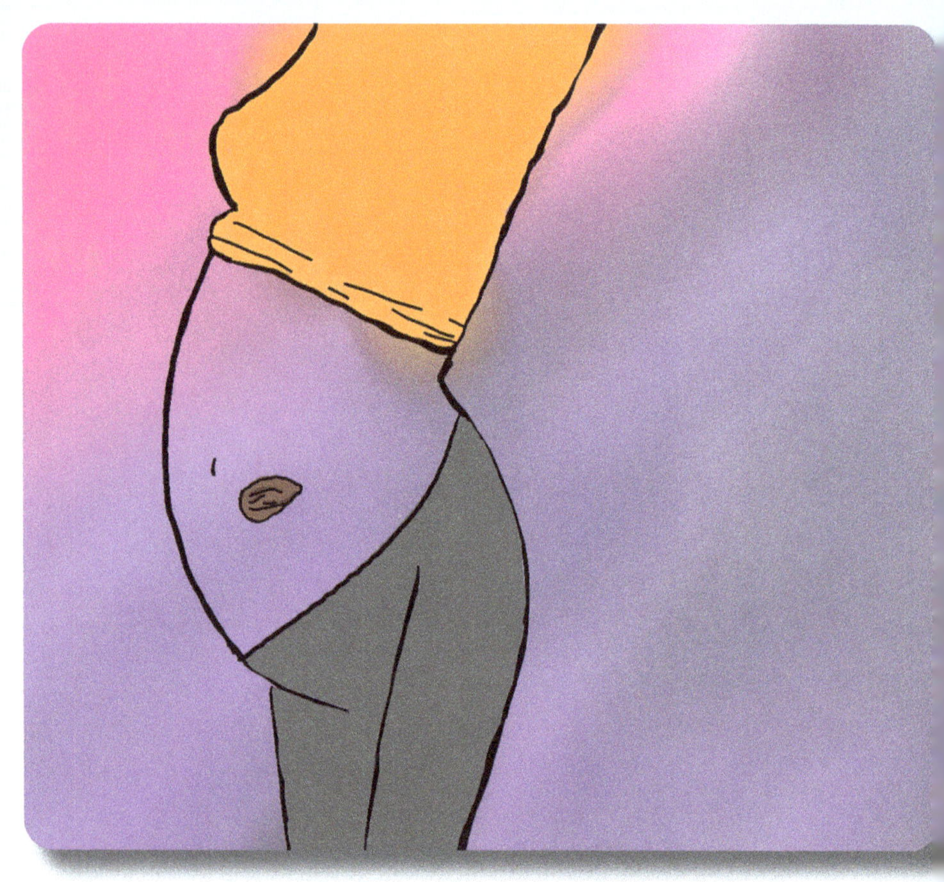

"The baby in Mommy's tummy
was like the seeds that didn't sprout. It
just wasn't the time for her to bloom,"
Daddy said.

I felt sad. I didn't know what to say.
I wish the baby wouldn't have stopped
growing. I wanted to be a big sister. I
didn't like seeing Mommy and Daddy
upset.

I think Daddy could tell I was sad. He hugged me tightly and whispered into my ear, "Make sure to give Mommy lots of hugs and love, okay? That's the best thing to do when someone, especially someone you love, is sad- just let them know you love them."

I gave Daddy a tight hug back and then went to go find Mommy. I found her in the baby's nursery, crying. When she saw me, she wiped her tears.

"Hey, sweetie," she tried to smile. "Can I help you with something?"

I said nothing, but went up to her, wrapped my arms around her, and gave her the biggest hug I possibly could.

Mommy picked me up and hugged me. "I'm lucky to have you," she said, starting to cry again.

I kissed her cheek. I was lucky to have her too.